BORN TO RUN

A Racehorse Grows Up

By Neil Johnson

SCHOLASTIC INC.
New York Toronto London Auckland Sydney

Special thanks to the people of Franks Farms, Inc.,
and Louisiana Downs racetrack.

ISBN 0-590-42836-5

Published by Scholastic Inc.

12 11 10 9 8 7 6 5 4 3 2 9/8 0 1 2 3 4/9

PRINTED IN THE U.S.A. 08

To Righton Elizabeth

There are many kinds of horses. Most racehorses are *thoroughbred horses.* The thoroughbred is a special horse born to run. This is the story of how a thoroughbred racehorse grows up.

Most thoroughbreds are born in the springtime and are almost always born in the safety of a barn. The mother horse, called a *mare*, lies down just before giving birth. It is usually very late at night or very early in the morning while it is still dark outside. Often a person specially trained to help will be in the stall with the mare. The baby horse, called a *foal*, usually comes out headfirst. In only a few minutes the foal is able to stand up on its own feet.

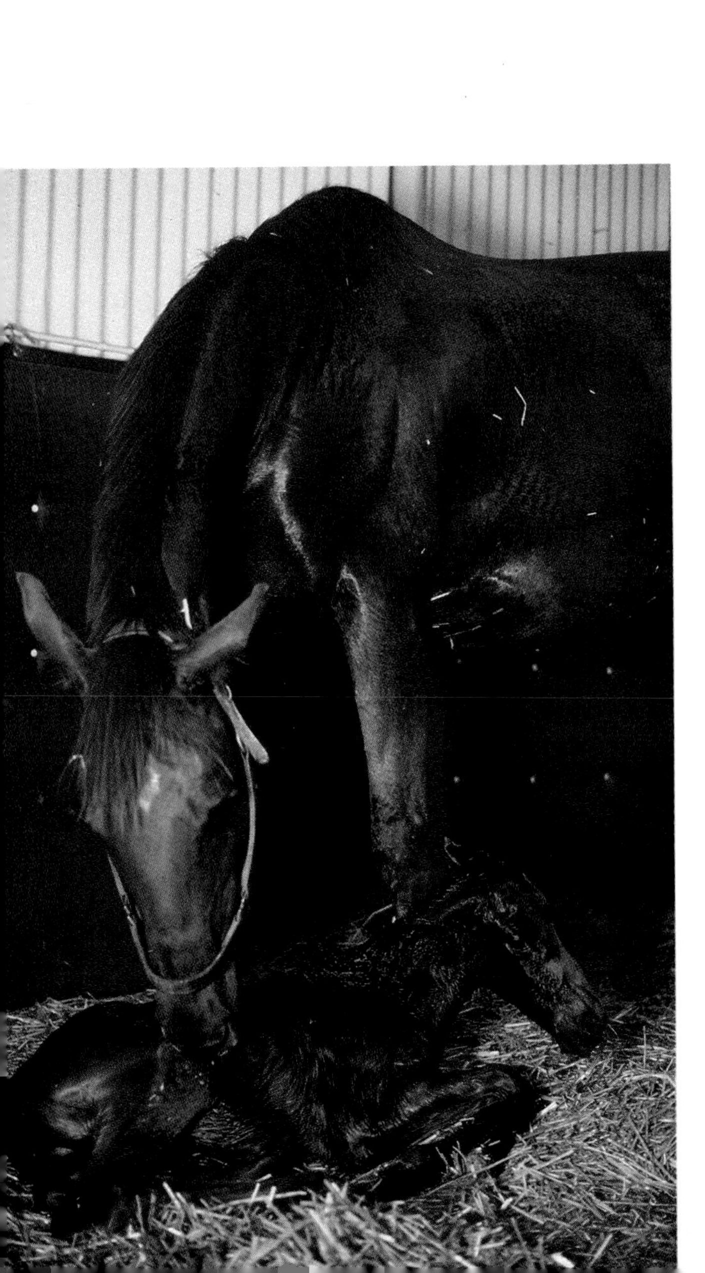

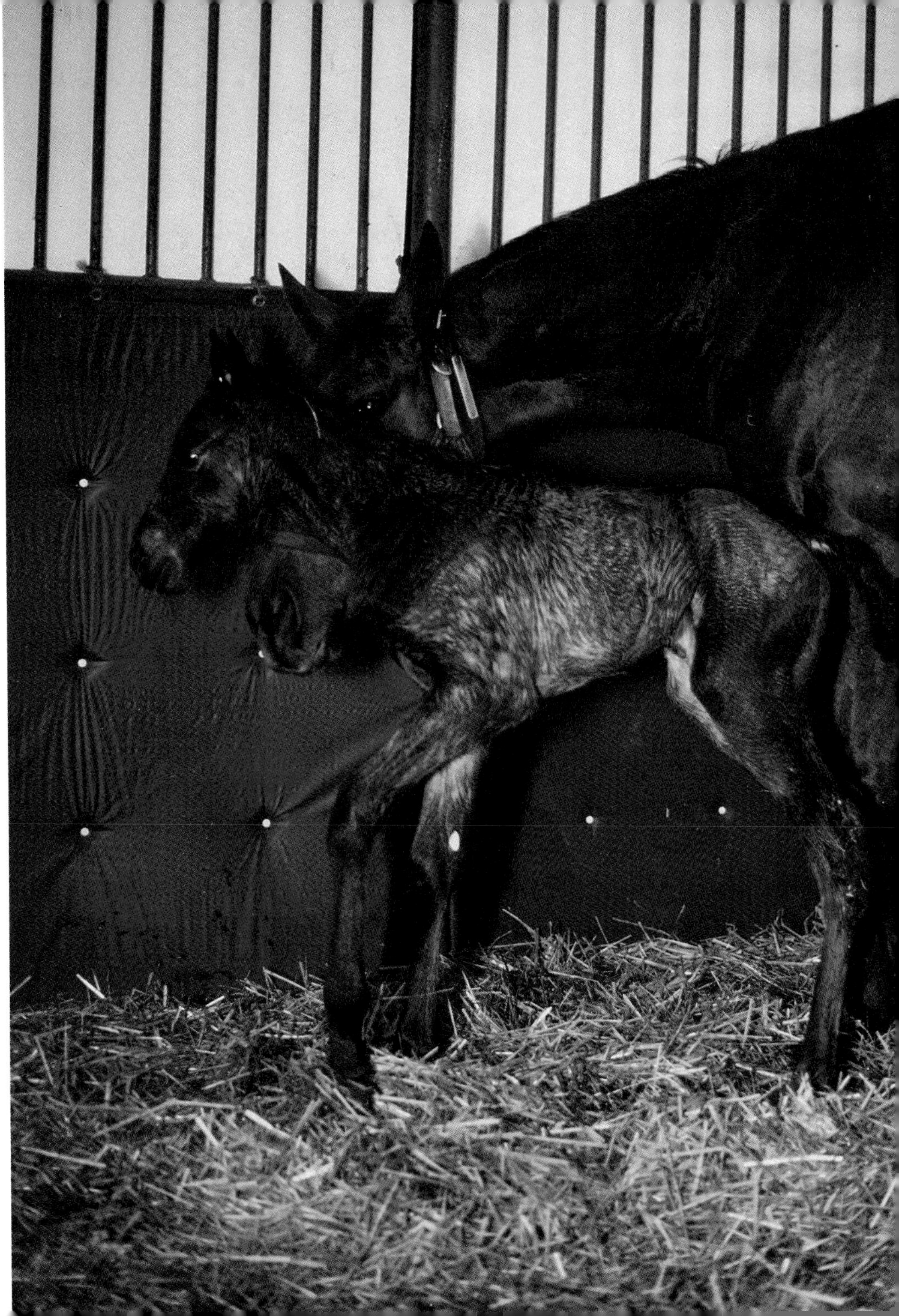

The foal needs time to learn to walk and nurse. So for the first few days, it must stay in the stall with its mother. But soon the foal and mare are put outside in a big, open grassy field. Here there are many other mares, each with one foal.

Like every baby, each foal is different in its own way. Some are frisky and playful; others are quiet and shy. Some like to play with the other foals, and some prefer to be alone. But every foal learns to run and to rest, and to eat oats and grass, and drink water just as its mother does.

After about six months, the foals and mares must be separated. This is called *weaning*. Once the foals are away from their mothers, they are called *weanlings*. At first, the young horses do not like being away from their mothers. But now they must learn to depend on themselves and on the people who will care for them as they grow up.

Young male horses are called *colts*. Young female horses are called *fillies*. Some time after weaning, the fillies and colts are separated. Colts and fillies grow up differently. Colts often play rough. They can accidentally hurt the gentler fillies. It is best to let them play and grow up apart.

All through the fall and winter the weanlings romp and play in the fields. They grow very quickly now, developing strong legs and firm muscles.

The first of January is a birthday for every thoroughbred horse. Every weanling born the spring before is considered one year old on that day. After January first, the weanlings are called *yearlings*. But they still have six months of growing up to do before they can begin racing school. For most thoroughbreds, school begins in the fall before their second birthday.

A *trainer* is a horse teacher. Trainers teach thoroughbreds how to use their natural abilities to become racehorses. Like all good teachers, they are patient with their students. They know that every lesson is a new experience for the young horses. Yearlings receive much attention and care from their trainers. A nervous horse soon finds that the trainer is its friend.

When racing school begins, the first thing the horse learns is how to walk with a person and take commands.

"Left!" "Right!" "Stop!"

The trainer uses his voice along with soft tugs on a rope.

Next, the yearling must get used to having a saddle on its back. When the horse is ready to carry weight for the first time, someone gently lies across its back. This is a new feeling and can be a little bit scary. But, slowly the young horse gets used to it.

It is very important for a racehorse to learn to take commands and to carry weight on its back.

Soon an *exercise rider* sits up in the saddle. By this time the yearling knows that the weight of a person on its back will not hurt it. The rider begins giving commands. The commands are familiar from the earlier lessons.

"Left!" "Right!" "Stop!"

The rider is also giving these commands through the *reins*, the leather straps which go to the horse's mouth and are held in the rider's hands. The rider practices with the horse first in the corral, then on trails, and finally on a *training track*.

On the training track, young horses are always exercised with other horses. They begin by walking and trotting in groups. They are not yet ready to run fast in a race. They must learn to move along the track slowly at first without stopping to play along the way. They must also learn to keep going even though something may distract or frighten them for a moment.

When the trainer decides a young horse is ready, he begins to let the horse run fast a little at a time. Then the trainer lets the horse run fast for longer stretches. This fast running is called *breezing*. Sometimes the exercise rider will breeze the horse alone and sometimes alongside another horse.

The trainer must not let the horse run too fast at first. If a young horse runs too fast, it will tire quickly. There are many things to learn about racing. It is especially important for a racehorse to know when to relax and when to run as

After a morning workout, it is time to go back to the barn. The stall in the barn is the horse's home. Here the *groom* takes care of it. Upon returning from practice at the training track, the groom first removes the bridle and saddle, called the *tack*. Then the groom gives the horse a cool bath and feeds it oats and hay.

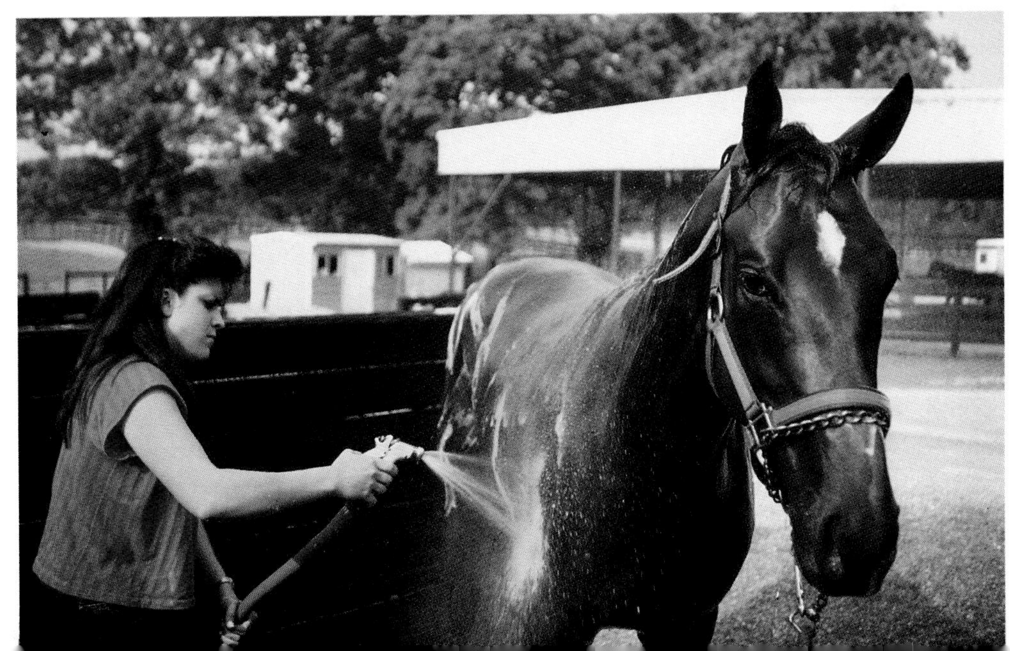

After their second January first, the yearlings are called *two-year-olds*. Some may be ready to race, and some may need more training. If the trainer decides a two-year-old is ready, it is time to go to the *racetrack*. The racetrack is a lot like the training track. Most are made of dirt, but some are grass or *turf*. At the racetrack, people come to watch the horses race and to bet on the horses they think will win.

The person who rides the horse at the racetrack is called the *jockey*. Jockeys are small because small people are easier for the horses to carry. The racehorse can run faster carrying a lighter weight rider. The colorful silk clothes the jockey wears are called *silks*. The different colors and patterns of silks worn by the jockey show who owns the horse the jockey is riding.

After a few practice or *training races*, it is time for a real race. Just before the first race, the horse notices changes. It gets less to eat for one thing, and it is not allowed to drink water at all. It will get plenty to eat and drink as soon as it cools down after the race is over.

There is much noise all around as the grandstand fills with people. Everyone is very excited to see the first race. Sometimes all the excitement makes the horses a bit nervous.

Before the race begins, each racehorse is ridden by a jockey to the *starting gate*. The jockeys try to keep their horses as calm as possible until the race begins. When the starting gates spring open, a loud bell rings. The race has begun! The horses burst out with the jockeys holding on tightly. After the first jump, the jockeys take control of the race. They must decide exactly when to speed the horse up and when to pass another horse. Everything the horse has learned in racing school will help it run the race.

Around the track, the jockeys guide the running horses. Racehorses run fast throughout the race. But not until the *home stretch*, the last part of the race on the straight part of the track, do the jockeys urge them to run as fast as they possibly can. The first horse under the wire—the *finish line*—wins!

APPROX ODDS
RACE
POST TIME
MAIN TRACK
FAST
GRASS TRACK
FIRM
POOL TOTALS
WIN
PLACE
SHOW
1 2 3 4 5 6 7 8 9 10 11 12
RESULT WIN PLACE SHOW

Every thoroughbred horse is different. Some are especially smart. Some are trained especially well. But not all of them learn to run fast in a race. And some who can run fast may not have the desire to run faster than all the other horses. Not every horse can be a winner. Those that do win, have a special winning spirit, called *heart*. To win a race, the best kind of horse to have is a horse with heart.

In many ways every thoroughbred horse is a winner. Strength, grace, and intelligence are in its blood. And even if a thoroughbred never sees a racetrack, it was still born to run with a spirit and beauty that few animals can ever equal.